A Kitten Called Holly

Toffee sprang out of the Christmas tree, knocking over Mum's vase of flowers. The water spilled on to Holly and Ivy. The drenched kittens howled in shock and started running madly around the room. The door opened and Dad appeared, holding a bunch of carrots. "What on earth is going on?"

Also by

HELEN PETERS

LOOK OUT FOR:

A Piglet Called Truffle

A Duckling Called Button

A Sheepdog Called Sky

A Lamb Called Lucky

FOR OLDER READERS:

The Secret Hen House Theatre

The Farm Beneath the Water

Evie's Ghost

A Kitten Called Holly

HELEN PETERS

illustrated by
ELLIE SNOWDON

nosy crow

First published in the UK in 2017 by Nosy Crow Ltd
The Crow's Nest, 14 Baden Place,
Crosby Row, London SE1 1YW

1 3 5 7 9 10 8 6 4 2

A CIP catalogue record for this book will be available from the British Library.

Printed and bound in the UK by Clays Ltd, St. Ives Plc

Papers used by Nosy Crow are made from wood grown in
sustainable forests.

ISBN: 978 0 85763 963 9

www.nosycrow.com

For Jimmy, Patrick and Megan
H. P.

For my sister, Lizzie
E. S.

Chapter One
It Sounds Really Fierce

"This is perfect," said Jasmine, smiling at her best friend, Tom. "Come in, Sky, and don't make a sound. We have to keep it secret from Manu."

Jasmine's collie dog, Sky, wagged his tail and padded into the shed. Jasmine pulled the door shut. It was coming off its hinges and the rotting wood dragged along the ground. It clearly hadn't been shut properly for years.

"Sit, Sky," said Jasmine, and Sky obediently sat on the dusty floor.

"I can't believe we've never been in here

before," said Tom. "It will be really cosy when we've cleaned it up. Look, it's even got a window."

"We can bring out some old chairs," said Jasmine, "and find something for a table. And we can clear all the junk out."

The shed was a small brick building with a sloping roof, in the garden of the farmhouse where Jasmine lived. Two rusting oil stoves stood in one corner, next to a tangled bundle of wire and a collapsed straw bale. On a rough wooden shelf sat a couple of dusty old jam jars containing screws and nails.

"Look," said Tom, "there's a mouse skeleton on the floor. Manu would love that for his collection."

"We can give it to him as a present," said Jasmine. Her six-year-old brother, Manu, kept a gruesome collection of animal bones and skulls in his bedroom. "But we won't tell him where we got it. This clubhouse is our secret."

2

"That shelf will be perfect for books," said
Tom. "And we can put our maps of the rescue
centre up on the wall."

It was a Friday afternoon in late October
and they had a two-week half term holiday
stretching out in front of them. Jasmine and Tom
were planning to run an animal rescue centre
when they grew up, and their new clubhouse
was where they were going to work out all the
details.

"What shall we call the club?" asked Jasmine.

"The Animal Rescue Club," said Tom.

Jasmine screwed up her nose. "Not very original." Then her eyes lit up. "Oh, but it's A.R.C. for short! Arc. Like Noah's Ark."

"Exactly," said Tom. "So it's where abandoned animals come to be safe. Like you, Sky."

He reached down to stroke Sky's silky fur, and Sky wagged his feathery tail across the floor.

Four months ago, Jasmine had found Sky abandoned and left to die in a hedge. She had nursed him back to health and now he was completely devoted to her. Jasmine and Tom had also rescued a clutch of orphaned duck eggs from the riverbank in the spring, after a dog had killed the mother duck. The surviving duckling, Button, was now a fully-grown drake, who lived happily with the free-range chickens. And Jasmine's very first rescue animal had been a tiny runt piglet that she had found on a neighbouring farm. She had called the piglet Truffle, and the sick little runt had turned into a giant sow, who

4

lived in the orchard behind the farmhouse.

"I'm not allowed to keep any more animals," said Jasmine. "Mum and Dad made me promise that if I rescue any more, I have to rehome them."

"Will you still be able to look after my guinea pigs at Christmas?" asked Tom.

"Of course I will," said Jasmine. "Are you going to your granny's in Cornwall again?"

"Yes," said Tom. "It's going to be great. She makes the best Christmas dinner ever. And we're going to swim in the sea on Christmas morning."

"Swim in the *sea*? On Christmas Day?" said Jasmine. "Are you crazy?"

Tom was about to reply when something thudded against the door. Then came frantic scratching on the wood and an ear-piercing yowl.

The children looked at each other in alarm.

"Sounds like a cat," whispered Jasmine.

"A really angry cat," said Tom.

"Maybe it's a wild cat," said Jasmine, "and it's been living in this shed. And now we've shut the door and it can't get in."

The cat continued to yowl and scratch at the door.

"We could tame it and have it as our club mascot," said Tom. "If it's living here, it kind of belongs to the club anyway."

"That's a brilliant idea," said Jasmine. "And I wouldn't be keeping an animal, because this is its home already."

"I wonder what it looks like," said Tom.

They tried to peer through the cracks in the door, but the gaps were too narrow and they couldn't see the cat.

"We need to let it in," said Jasmine, "if it lives here."

"We'd better stand well back," said Tom.

"I don't think it will hurt us. It's probably just confused because the door's shut."

Tom looked doubtful. "I don't know. It sounds really fierce."

"It'll be fine," said Jasmine confidently. She pushed the door open.

Into the shed shot a screaming bundle of grey fur. It hurled itself at Jasmine, hissing and spitting. She screamed and covered her face with her hands as the cat leapt up at her, scratching and biting. Jasmine screeched in pain and, with a final terrific yowling, the cat sprang down and bolted out of the shed.

"Are you all right?" asked Tom, sounding shaken.

Jasmine sat heavily on the collapsing bale behind her. She looked at her hands. They had deep red

scratches all along them, and there were sharp
teeth marks on her right hand.

"That must really hurt," said Tom.

Jasmine clutched her hands together to try to
stop the pain. "That cat really didn't want us to
be here. Ow, my hands sting so much."

"You need to run them under the tap," said
Tom. "Let's go indoors."

Jasmine frowned. "What was that?"

"What?"

"That funny squeaking sound."

"I didn't hear anything."

"Listen," said Jasmine.

They listened. Birds tweeted in the garden.
Sheep baaed in the field. From the orchard came
Truffle's low contented grunt.

"I can't hear anything," said Tom. "Let's go."

They stepped out into the sunny garden,
avoiding the prickly leaves of the holly bush
beside the shed. Then Jasmine heard it again:
a high-pitched sound, somewhere between

8

squeaking and mewing.

She turned to Tom. His expression showed her that he had heard it too.

"What is it?" he whispered.

"I don't know," said Jasmine, "but there's something in there."

They crept back into the half-light of the shed. There was another squeaking sound.

"It's coming from behind that bale," said Tom.

The baler twine that had held the straw together had broken, so that much of the straw had collapsed in a messy heap. The children peered over the bale into the dark corner.

Jasmine gasped in delight. "Kittens!" she whispered. "Oh, they're so cute!"

"Three of them," said Tom, grinning with excitement. "They're tiny."

The kittens were cuddled up together in a deep nest of straw. One was a tabby, one was ginger and the third was black. The tabby kitten and the ginger one lay still, but the black kitten was crawling over its littermates, mewing.

"They're gorgeous," said Jasmine. "I wonder how old they are."

"They can't be newborn," said Tom, "because their eyes are open."

"So they must be at least a week old. I don't think they're much older than that. They're so little."

The black kitten gave another piercing mew.

"It wants its mother," said Tom. And then he drew in his breath and looked at Jasmine in horror.

"Oh no," said Jasmine. "That cat. She must be their mother."

"We shut her out from her kittens," said Tom. "And now we've frightened her away."

Chapter Two

What If She Doesn't Come Back?

"That's why she was so fierce," said Jasmine. "She thought we were threatening her babies."

"We need to get her back," said Tom. "If she can't feed the kittens, they'll die."

They walked out into the garden, looking for the cat. But there was no sign of her.

"How are we going to get her back?" said Tom. "She's completely wild. She's not going to come if we call her, is she?"

Jasmine thought for a second. Then she said, "Food. All animals come for food. And she must be really hungry if she's feeding kittens."

They ran up the garden path and in through the back door of the farmhouse to the scullery. Jasmine had two cats of her own, Toffee and Marmite, and their food was kept in the cupboard next to the sink. She grabbed two pouches from the box and some empty takeaway containers from the next cupboard.

"We'll use these as bowls," she said. "We can lay a trail of food across the garden, leading up to the shed. That should tempt her back."

In the garden, Jasmine tore the top off the first pouch and started squeezing it into a container.

"Don't put too much in each one," said Tom, "or she'll be full before she gets to the shed."

They put a little food in each container and laid them in a line from the bottom of the garden to the shed. Then they tiptoed in to look at the kittens. The black kitten was still mewing piteously.

"Do you think we should give them some

12

milk?" asked Tom.

"Kittens can't have cows' milk," said Jasmine. "It upsets their stomachs. I wish Mum or Dad was here. They'd know what to do."

Jasmine's dad was a farmer and her mum was a vet. Dad was out in the fields feeding his calves and Mum was working at the vet's surgery.

"You could phone the surgery," said Tom. "Even if your mum can't speak to you, one of the nurses would know what to do, wouldn't they?"

"Good idea," said Jasmine. "Let's do that now."

"Should I stay here," Tom asked, "and keep an eye on the kittens?"

"They should be OK for a bit. And the mother won't come back if we're here. We should leave them alone so she feels safe to return."

"Hopefully she'll smell the food," said Tom, "and she won't be able to resist."

"What did Linda say?" asked Tom, when Jasmine

put the phone down. Linda was the head nurse at Mum's surgery.

"Well, we need to take away the food bowls near the shed," said Jasmine. "Come on."

"Why?" asked Tom, as they ran down the garden path.

"She said it's good to leave food out, but it should be at least three metres from the nest. The mother won't go back to the kittens if there's food nearby, because she won't want to attract other cats to her nest."

Tom picked up the food bowl in the shed. "And what about the kittens?" he asked.

Jasmine took the bowl they had left outside the door. "Linda said we should leave them. Their mother has to go off hunting, so they're used to being alone for short periods. And they can survive for several hours as long as they're warm and dry."

Tom looked worried. "But the mother was probably coming back from hunting when we scared her away. She might already have been out for hours."

Jasmine stared at him anxiously. "I hadn't thought of that."

"So what should we do?" asked Tom.

"I don't know. We definitely shouldn't touch them. The mother won't like it if there's a strange scent on them. Linda said she might move them anyway now, since we've disturbed her nesting place." Jasmine looked at Tom and saw that he felt as guilty as she did.

"But what if she doesn't come back?" asked Tom. "They won't survive on their own for much longer."

"Linda said we should watch from a distance to see if she comes. Let's get a rug and wait on the other side of the garden."

"And if she doesn't come?" said Tom.

"I don't know. But I'm sure she will. They're her babies, after all. She's bound to come back."

Jasmine tried to sound confident,

but inside she felt horribly worried. What if the mother cat never returned? Then she and Tom would be responsible for orphaning three tiny kittens, not to mention causing terrible distress to the poor mother.

They fetched a rug from the cupboard under the stairs and sat by the hedge on the other side of the garden. They waited for what seemed like hours. As dusk fell, the colours of the garden faded and the world began to turn to shades of grey.

"I'm freezing," Jasmine whispered.

"Me too," said Tom. "I wish I had gloves."

Jasmine thought about going inside to fetch gloves and a warmer coat, but she was afraid to move in case the cat was nearby and she accidentally frightened her away again.

Why wasn't Mum home from work yet? Jasmine checked her watch and was amazed to find that only twenty-five minutes had passed since they had sat down.

Then Tom nudged her. "Look," he whispered.

Slinking silently through the shadows by the hedge was the mother cat. She slipped inside the shed.

Jasmine felt her shoulders drop with relief, and realised that she must have been hunching them all this time.

"Phew," said Tom. "I was so worried. Those poor kittens must be so hungry. I bet they're pleased to see her." He stood up and rubbed his hands together. "I'm freezing. Let's go in."

But Jasmine was still watching the shed. "Wait," she said.

"Why?"

"Remember what Linda said? The mother might take them away."

Tom frowned. "She wouldn't really, would she?"

But he turned to look at the shed. And at that moment, the cat came padding out through the doorway, carrying a kitten in her mouth.

"Oh, no," said Jasmine. "She *is* moving them."

"We should follow her," murmured Tom. "See where she goes. Come on."

Jasmine grabbed the hem of his coat. "No," she whispered. "We might scare her even further away. And she might not come back for the others if she knows we're nearby. Let's just watch from here."

Tom sat down. They watched the cat as she slunk back along the hedgerow. Near the bottom of the garden, she disappeared behind a bush. They kept looking but she didn't reappear.

"She's gone through the hedge into the fields,"

said Tom. "She might be going miles away."

"She's got to come back for the other two, though," said Jasmine.

"How about when she comes back for the next one, we just creep down the garden on this side?" said Tom. "She won't see us from over there, and we might find out where she's going."

So when the cat padded back a few minutes later and fetched the second kitten, Tom and Jasmine stood up very quietly and crept down their side of the garden, keeping pace with her. When she disappeared behind the bush again, they moved slightly further down, so they would see her come out on the other side.

The cat emerged from behind the bush and padded on towards the bottom of the garden, the kitten dangling from her mouth by the scruff of its neck. When she reached the hedge, she didn't take her kitten through it, as they had feared she would. Instead, she made for the rickety old wooden tool shed in the far corner of the garden. The door was shut, but there was a gap at the bottom of the wall where one of the planks had rotted away. The cat squeezed through the gap and disappeared into the shed.

Jasmine grinned at Tom. "That's perfect!" she whispered. "She's stayed in the garden!"

Tom looked excited. "We can leave food out for her, and then she'll grow tame, and we'll be able to play with the kittens."

"Jasmine, Tom, are you out there?" called Jasmine's mum from the top of the garden.

"Quick," whispered Jasmine, "before she shouts again and scares the cat away."

"There you are," said Mum, as they ran up the path. "What are you doing out here without coats on? You must be frozen. Come in for dinner. It's all ready."

"We have to stay out a little bit longer," said Jasmine. "It's an emergency." And she quickly told her mother the whole story.

"Well, it sounds as though everything's fine," said Mum. "The cat's moving her kittens to a safe place."

"But she hasn't moved the third kitten yet. We need to make sure she comes back for it."

"There's no reason to suppose she won't," said Mum. "You can check after dinner. Dad's made spaghetti bolognese."

The mention of her favourite dinner reminded Jasmine how cold and hungry she was. She and Tom followed Mum up the path.

"We'll come out straight afterwards," said Jasmine, "and check she's taken the third kitten."

"And if she has," said Tom, "we can start sorting out the clubhouse."

"Two whole weeks of holidays," said Jasmine. "We can make the clubhouse amazing."

22

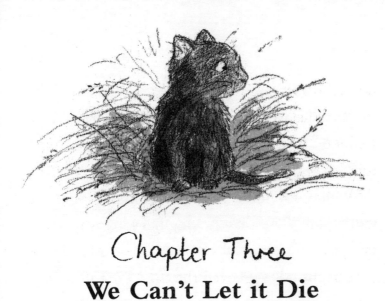

Chapter Three
We Can't Let it Die

In the farmhouse kitchen, Dad was serving out
the dinner. Manu and his best friend, Ben, were
sitting at the table, sucking spaghetti noisily into
their mouths. Jasmine's sixteen-year-old sister,
Ella, was also there, a book propped open in
front of her.

"How was your school outing, boys?" asked
Mum. Manu's class had spent the day at a local
museum, learning about the King Charles the
Second.

Manu grinned. "It was so cool," he said. "We

saw a dead fox on the road. It was all squashed in the middle where a car had run over it."

"Ugh," said Jasmine. "That's disgusting."

"And what about the museum?" asked Mum.

"Lunch was really good," said Manu. "Noah didn't like his sandwiches, so we swapped, and his mum uses this really soft white bread that you can squidge into balls and throw at people. You should buy that sort of bread, Mum."

"So what did you learn about King Charles the Second?" asked Dad.

Both boys looked blank. "What?"

"King Charles the Second. Isn't that who you were supposed to be learning about?"

"Oh, we didn't really listen to that bit," said Manu. "We were playing with this bit of playdough Ben found in his pocket."

"Everyone was sitting on the floor cross-legged," said Ben, "and we were sticking little blobs of playdough on the bottom of people's shoes in front of us. So when they stood up their

24

shoes were all sticky on the floor and they didn't know why. It was so funny."

"Great," said Dad. "Excellent. Time well spent, then."

"What if the kitten's still there when we go back?" asked Jasmine.

Ella looked up from her book. "What kitten?"

"We found a nest of kittens," Jasmine said.

"Where?" asked Manu, an excited gleam in his eyes.

Tom shot Jasmine a warning look.

"Just in the farmyard," said Jasmine vaguely. "In one of the buildings. Anyway, the cat's moved them now."

"But you said a kitten might still be there," said Manu.

"Mum said the mother will have come back and fetched it," said Jasmine.

"Me and Ben will find them," said Manu.

"No, you mustn't," said Jasmine in alarm. "If you disturb them, the cat will move them again."

25

Jasmine ate her dinner as quickly as she could. As soon as Tom put the last of his spaghetti in his mouth, she said, "Please may we leave the table?"

"Where are you going?" asked Manu.

"Just up to my room."

She and Tom left the kitchen. But they didn't go upstairs. Instead, Jasmine fetched a torch from the hall cupboard while Tom opened the front door as quietly as he could. Then they crept out into the dark garden.

They didn't expect to find anything in their clubhouse. The mother cat had had plenty of time to collect the third kitten. But as they drew near to the shed, they heard a high-pitched mewing.

"Oh, no," said Jasmine. "She hasn't come back."

They tiptoed inside. Jasmine shone the torch to one side of the nest so as not to frighten the kitten by shining a light directly into its eyes.

There, all alone, was the little black kitten. It was clearly distressed, crawling around in the

straw, mewing urgently and continuously. Tears
sprang to Jasmine's eyes as she watched it.

"We have to take it to its mother," she said.

"We can't," said Tom. "You said if she finds our
scent on it, she'll reject it."

"But look at it. It will die soon if it doesn't get
fed."

"We should leave," said Tom. "She might be
coming back right now."

"I don't think she's going to come," said
Jasmine. "She collected the second one right
after the first, didn't she? Why has she left this
one so long?"

Tom was silent for a minute. Then he said, "Let's ask your mum what we should do."

Jasmine leaned over and spoke to the kitten. "We'll be back in a minute, little one. We're going to find out how to help you."

To their relief, Manu and Ben had left the kitchen by the time they got there. Mum and Dad were clearing the table. When Jasmine explained the situation, Mum looked thoughtful.

"I'm afraid it sounds as though the mother has rejected this one," she said. "Was it mewing when you first saw them?"

"Yes," said Tom. "The other two were lying there peacefully, but the black one was crawling around and mewing."

"Hmm," said Mum. "So the mother had probably already rejected it. If the other two were quiet and content, they were probably well fed, but it sounds as though the black one was already hungry."

"Should we take it to the mother?" asked Jasmine.

Mum shook her head. "No. If you take back the one she's rejected, she might reject the others, too."

"So what should we do?" asked Jasmine. "If we leave it, it will die."

Mum and Dad exchanged a look. Jasmine glanced at Tom, and saw her own excitement mirrored in his face.

"We can't let it die, can we?" said Tom.

Dad looked at Tom and then at Jasmine. "Clearly this kitten needs to be looked after," he said. "So I guess you'd better bring it indoors."

"Calm down, you two," said Mum, as Tom and Jasmine shrieked with excitement. "You can bring the kitten in and look after it, but we're not having any more pets, Jasmine. You already have two cats, a dog, a pig and a duck. As soon as the kitten's old enough, we're going to find a home for it. Do you understand?"

Jasmine looked despondent. But she said, "Yes, I understand."

"And you promise me

you won't beg and pester to
keep it?"

"I promise. Come on, Tom,
let's go and get our new kitten!"

As they ran down the
garden path, Jasmine turned
to Tom. "I know I can't keep
the kitten," she said, "but
you could."

"I wish I could," said Tom, "but Mum hates animals in the house. She only let me have the guinea pigs because they live in the garden. There's no way she'd let me have a cat. I've asked her loads of times, but she'll never change her mind."

Chapter Four
We're Going to Look After You

The black kitten was mewing more piteously than ever when the children got back to the shed. Tom held the torch while Jasmine reached down and gently scooped up the tiny animal. It looked at her with its enormous blue eyes and mewed desperately.

"It hardly weighs anything," she said, stroking the kitten's silky-soft fur.

Tom cupped his hands. "Can I hold it?"

Jasmine sat the tiny kitten in Tom's hands. "I wonder if it's a boy or a girl," she said. "Mum will be able to tell."

"Hello, little kitten," said Tom. "You're so lovely."

"It's starving," said Jasmine. "Come on. We need to give it milk."

"I thought you said they couldn't have milk," Tom said, as they hurried back to the house.

"Not cows' milk. It probably needs a special kitten formula. I hope Mum's got some in the car."

The boot of Mum's car was always crammed with boxes of equipment and medicines for treating sick animals. As they got back to the kitchen, Mum came in through the other door, holding a plastic container with a picture of a cat on one side.

"Oh, great," said Jasmine, grabbing the tub. "You've got kitten milk."

"Calm down, Jasmine," said Mum. "There's no need to snatch."

"But it's an emergency. The kitten's starving."

34

Mum smiled at the mewling kitten. "What a sweet little thing."

Jasmine scanned the writing on the container, looking for instructions on how to prepare the formula.

"It's so cute," said Tom, stroking the kitten. "Why would the mum reject it?"

"I was going to talk to you both about that," said Mum, as Jasmine opened the tub and took out the measuring scoop. "I know it's impossible not to get attached to a beautiful kitten, but the problem is that nature often does know best."

Jasmine didn't like the sound of this. "What do you mean?"

"I mean that when a cat rejects her kitten, she often does it for a reason. This kitten might not be completely healthy. It might have something wrong with it that isn't obvious yet. I just want you to be prepared, that's all."

"Prepared for what?" asked Jasmine. "Are you saying the kitten might die?"

As Mum started to reply, her work phone rang. She pulled it from her pocket and walked into the hall to answer it.

Jasmine was used to conversations ending abruptly every time Mum's phone rang. It always meant an animal emergency of some kind and, if Mum was on call, she had to drop everything and go.

"Sorry, you two," Mum said, when she reappeared. "I've got to go and see a horse over at Selham. Use a syringe to feed the kitten – very slowly, just a few drops at a time, because if the milk goes in too fast, it could go into the windpipe. I'll get you a proper feeding bottle tomorrow. Dad's in his office if you need anything."

Jasmine was measuring the powdered milk into a jam jar. "Could you just tell us if the kitten's a boy or a girl?" she asked.

Mum examined the kitten. "She's a girl," she said. "And you're very beautiful, aren't you?"

She smiled at the kitten and handed her back
to Tom. "Keep her warm," she said. "That's really
important. And make sure she's on her tummy
in a sitting position when you feed her. Now I
must shoot off." She kissed the top of Jasmine's
head, grabbed her car keys and left.

Jasmine held the measuring scoop under the
hot tap. "Two parts water to one part formula,"
she said. She tipped two scoops of water into the
jar, screwed on the lid and shook it hard. "That's
quite a lot, but we can keep the rest in the fridge
and warm up a bit for each feed."

Tom was studying the side of the formula tub.
"We need to weigh her," he said. "It says you
have to feed them 8cc per ounce of weight every
twenty-four hours. How much is 8cc?"

"It should say on the syringe," said Jasmine.
"I'll go and get one."

When she returned from the scullery with
a plastic syringe, the little kitten was sitting in
the kitchen scale pan, her blue eyes huge and

frightened.

"Six ounces," said Tom. He lifted her out and held her against his jumper. "After we've fed her, I'll make a proper chart, and we can write down her weight and how much she eats every day, like we did with Sky."

He took a notepad and pencil from the dresser. "So 8cc per ounce of weight means eight times six. How often does it say we should feed her?"

Jasmine consulted the side of the tub. "Every three hours."

"Through the night as well?"

"I guess so," said Jasmine. "We'll have to set the alarm." Tom was staying for a sleepover.

"Or we can just stay awake all night," said Tom.

Jasmine smiled. "That's a much better idea." She unscrewed the lid of the jar and swirled the milk around to check for lumps. "How much should we give her?"

"6cc per feed," said Tom, who had worked it out on the notepad.

Jasmine dipped the syringe into the jar and drew up the plunger. She pushed back her jumper sleeve and dropped a little milk on to her wrist to check it was at body temperature.

"Perfect," she said. "You're going to be fed now, little kitten."

She pushed the plunger down to the 6cc mark. "Do you want to feed her?" she asked Tom.

"You should do it," said Tom. "I got to hold her all this time. I'll read up about looking after her."

Jasmine sat down and Tom passed the mewing kitten to her. Jasmine moved her finger to the kitten's mouth to prise it open, but there was no need. The kitten opened her mouth and started to suck at her finger. Jasmine took the syringe and carefully dropped a little milk into her mouth.

The kitten moved her head around and batted at the syringe with her front paws. Jasmine used her free hand to keep the paws away as she tried to keep the syringe in the kitten's mouth and not spill the milk. It was hard to move the plunger slowly enough to only release a drop or two at a time.

"It will be much easier once we have a bottle," she said to Tom, when he returned with Mum's laptop. "But at least she's drinking. That's a good sign."

"What shall we call her?" asked Tom.

"You should name her," said Jasmine. "I named Sky and Button and Truffle."

Tom narrowed his eyes thoughtfully. "Hmm." He was silent for a minute and then he said, "Holly. I like that name. And there's a holly bush right outside the shed where we found her."

"Holly," said Jasmine. "That suits her." She looked into the kitten's blue eyes. "Hello, Holly. We're going to look after you."

Chapter Five
She'll Change Her Mind In the End

Manu came into the kitchen while Jasmine was giving Holly the last of her milk and Tom was reading advice online about looking after orphaned kittens.

"Are there any biscuits?" Manu asked. Then he saw Holly and his eyes lit up. "Oh, he's so cute! Can I hold him?"

"She's a girl," said Jasmine, "and she's called Holly. You can hold her when she's finished feeding."

"It says we need to burp her when she's

finished," said Tom. "Like a baby."

"I remember Mum doing that with Manu," said Jasmine. "You hold them over your shoulder and rub their back. It gets out the trapped wind." She turned to her brother. "I hope Holly's not like you. You used to throw up after every single feed."

"Have you got a shoebox?" Tom asked. "It says a shoebox lined with a towel is the best bed. And she needs a heat pad."

Jasmine frowned. "I don't think we've got one of those."

"Or you can use a hot water bottle. But that might be a bit big. She needs to be able to move away from it if she gets too hot."

"What about that mini hot water bottle you gave Dad last Christmas?" suggested Manu. "The one he puts in his coat pocket for a handwarmer?"

Jasmine looked at her brother in amazement. "That might be the first useful thing you've ever said."

Manu looked wounded. "I say useful things all the time. You just don't listen."

Jasmine handed Holly to Tom and rummaged in Dad's coat pockets for the mini hot water bottle.

"Actually, instead of a towel, we should use a blanket from the cats' basket," said Tom, still reading the website. "It's so that Holly will get used to Toffee and Marmite's scent."

"Manu!" shouted Ella from upstairs. "Why is the bathroom sink full of bones?"

Manu went to the doorway. "I was washing them," he shouted back.

"Well, come and get them out."

"In a bit," said Manu.

"Now!" shouted Ella.

Manu gave a heavy sigh and left the room.

"Here it is," said Jasmine, pulling the hot water bottle from one of Dad's coat pockets. She put the kettle on and went to fetch a shoebox.

 44

When she returned, Tom whispered, "Look, she's sleeping."

Jasmine looked. Holly was snuggled up in Tom's lap, her eyes closed, looking perfectly contented.

"She's so gorgeous," said Jasmine.

Tom scratched the back of his hand. "I've got bites," he said. "They're really itchy."

Jasmine looked at the little red marks and pulled a face. "Oh, dear," she said. "I think you've got fleas."

Tom looked horrified. "Fleas?"

"They must be from Holly," said Jasmine. "Never mind. We'll comb them out."

Tom was frantically scratching his arms. "Oh, no, I'm itchy all over now. My mum will go crazy if I have fleas."

Jasmine fetched the flea comb from the scullery. She knelt beside Tom and ran it through Holly's fur. Holly opened her eyes sleepily and closed them again.

"Sorry, Holly," said Jasmine, "but I'm going to have to comb every part of you. You just carry on sleeping."

"It did say on that website that you have to check feral cats for fleas," said Tom, "but Holly

looked so clean and silky that I didn't think she'd
have any."

"You can never tell," said Jasmine. "Fleas are so
small you hardly ever see them."

"What's a feral cat anyway?" asked Tom. "Does
it just mean a wild cat?"

"I think wild cats are a whole different
species," said Jasmine, "and feral cats are just
normal cats that don't have homes."

She wiped the comb on a piece of kitchen roll.
There were a few flecks of black on the white
paper. Jasmine held the paper under the tap and
dripped water on to it. The black specks turned
dark red. "Yep," she said. "Flea dirt. It's actually
dried blood, you see. Holly's blood, poor thing."

She combed the underside of Holly's tail and
then inspected the comb. "And there's a flea."

She crushed the flea in the paper. "You have to
be really vicious with them," she said. "They're
so tough, they can survive almost anything."

"My mum definitely won't let me have her

now," said Tom, "once she sees I've got flea bites."

"Don't let her see, then."

"She'll notice. She notices everything."

"But we can't let her go to another home," said Jasmine. "You'll have to convince her."

"I'll really try," he said. "I'll tell her there's nothing else I want for Christmas."

"That might work," said Jasmine. "Holly won't even cost anything. And if your mum won't budge, I'll persuade mine to let me keep her."

But when Mum came home, she wasn't in a persuadable mood. She wouldn't even let Jasmine and Tom set an alarm to give Holly a night feed.

"She's nearly two weeks' old, by the look of her," she said, "and she doesn't need feeding in the middle of the night. You can give her a late feed tonight, and you can get up early, but you're not setting your alarm for 2am."

"OK," said Jasmine.

They would just have to stay awake all night instead, she thought.

Mum looked at her suspiciously. "And if I hear a sound out of you after I've switched off your light, Holly will be going to a rescue centre in the morning."

Jasmine stared at her mother in horror. "You wouldn't do that!"

"Try me," said Mum. "I'm not having two exhausted children in the house tomorrow. If you want to look after her, you'll need your sleep."

"OK," said Jasmine again. But she had every intention of staying up all night. And Mum clearly didn't trust her, because she insisted on leaving Jasmine's bedroom door open after she had switched out the light, and then she went into her study next to Jasmine's room and left that door open too.

Tom and Jasmine lay silently in their beds, with Holly curled up in her shoebox on the floor between them, fast asleep with a tummy full of milk. They listened for the sound of Mum leaving her study, planning to get up as soon as she went downstairs. But Mum just carried on tapping at her computer. Was she ever going to stop working?

Chapter Six

So Lucky
We Found Her

Jasmine was woken by a little mewing noise. Her heart leapt with excitement. Holly!

It was pitch dark. She pressed the light button on her alarm clock.

Six thirty-six am.

Oh, no! They hadn't woken at two o'clock. Holly would be starving. They were terrible kitten owners.

Jasmine slipped out of bed. She could just see the shoebox in the shadows. She put her hand gently inside it and her fingers touched the kitten's soft warm fur. Holly gave another squeaky miaow. Jasmine stroked her and picked up the box. "I'm so sorry, Holly," she whispered. "I'm going to feed you right now."

As she was tiptoeing out of the room, she heard Tom stir. She turned.

"Jasmine?" he said sleepily.

Holly mewed again. Tom sat bolt upright.

"I'm going to feed her," said Jasmine.

"Wait, I'm coming," said Tom, scrambling out of bed.

They padded down to the kitchen. Jasmine fetched the milk and warmed it.

"Can I feed her?" asked Tom, lifting Holly out of her box. She was mewing continuously now.

"She's so hungry," said Jasmine. "I hope she wasn't mewing for ages before I woke up." She tested the milk on her wrist. "OK, this is the right temperature."

"Look," said Tom. "She's sucking my finger."

It didn't take long for Holly to drink her milk.

 52

Tom burped her, and then held her up to his face.

"All kittens are born with blue eyes," he said. "I read that last night. It said they start changing colour in a month. I wonder what colour Holly's will be."

"Maybe they'll stay blue," said Jasmine. She raised her finger a few centimetres in front of Holly's face and slowly moved it in a circle. Holly looked at it for a few seconds, and then she batted a tiny paw at it. Tom and Jasmine laughed.

"She's playing with us already!" said Jasmine. "That's a great sign."

Tom scratched the red bites on his hand. "We'd better flea-comb her again once she goes to sleep. And that won't be long. The website said kittens sleep for twenty hours a day."

Sure enough, a few minutes later, Holly fell asleep in Tom's lap. Jasmine went to get the flea comb. Toffee and Marmite looked up from their bed on the work surface as she came in to the scullery. Toffee jumped to the floor and rubbed himself against Jasmine's legs.

Tom and Jasmine had read last night about introducing older cats to a new kitten. Before you introduced them, you were supposed to get them used to each other's scents, as a cat's sense of smell is its most important sense for communication.

"Sorry you can't go in my room at the moment," said Jasmine, as she stroked Toffee's ginger fur. "Once you get to know Holly, you can go wherever you like again, but we need to take it slowly."

Toffee nuzzled at her hand, investigating the new scent.

"That's Holly you can smell," Jasmine told him. "We'll introduce you to her soon. I'm going to swap your blankets, so you'll get used to each other's scents. And remember, even though we have a new kitten, I still love you just as much as I always did, and I'll give you just as much attention as I always have."

After they had combed Holly and put her back in Jasmine's room, Jasmine said, "We should go and see if the other kittens are OK."

"But what if we disturb them," said Tom, "and the mother moves them again?"

"We'll tiptoe up really quietly and peep in the shed window. I just want to make sure they're all right. What if she's rejected them too?"

That settled it. They put on coats and wellies and went out to the garden. To their relief, the cat and her two remaining kittens were nestled together in a heap of empty paper sacks.

"They look so cute," said Tom. "Do you think they'll be OK? It's horrible to think what hard lives they might have, living in the wild."

"We won't let that happen," said Jasmine. "We're going to bring them indoors."

Tom stared at her. "Your mum will never let you."

"We have to persuade her," said Jasmine. "We'll make a plan. After all, she's a vet. She surely doesn't want to see animals suffering in her own back garden?"

When they went downstairs for breakfast, Mum was making scrambled eggs. Ella was sitting at the table, highlighting passages in her book. Tom and Jasmine sat opposite her.

"Morning, you two," said Mum. "How's Holly? I gather you've fed her, from the mess you left on the draining board."

"Sorry," said Jasmine. "I'll clear it up. She seems fine. Do you really think there's something wrong with her?"

"Don't worry, Jasmine," said Mum. "If she's eating well and she seems well, I expect she'll be fine. I'll give her a proper examination this morning, anyway."

"It was so lucky we found her, wasn't it, Tom?" said Jasmine, giving Tom a meaningful look. This was his cue to put their plan into action.

"Yes," said Tom. "Otherwise she'd have died. Eighty per cent of feral kittens die in their first year."

Ella looked up from her book, her eyes wide with alarm. "Eighty per cent?" she said. "Why?"

"Accidents or disease, usually," said Jasmine. "We've been reading about it. And the females can become pregnant at four months' old if they're not rescued. And then they're pregnant or rearing kittens their whole lives. It's so hard for them, and they can get terrible diseases."

"And they abandon their kittens, and then the kittens starve," said Tom. "It's awful."

"It is," said Mum. "That continual breeding cycle is no good at all. As soon as the kittens are weaned, we'll catch them in a humane trap and I'll neuter them and the cat. Then they'll have much healthier lives."

"And then can we bring them inside and tame them?" asked Jasmine.

Mum gave her a hard stare. "Jasmine, I've already told you we can't. This house is quite chaotic enough without two more feral kittens."

"We're not asking to keep them forever. Only

until they're tamed and old enough to go to new homes."

"I know it's hard to understand," said Mum, "but cats that haven't had human contact in their first few weeks of life are actually much happier living outdoors, as long as they have food and shelter. These ones are in an ideal situation. They can sleep in the shed, they'll have the whole farm to roam over, and you can put food and water out if you want to. Put it somewhere quiet and out of the way – under a bush or something. And do it in the daytime, not at night, so you don't get nocturnal wildlife taking it."

"But what if the kittens like us," said Jasmine, "and they want to be pets?"

"Jasmine, I've said you can rear Holly and you can feed the others. I think that's quite enough, don't you?"

Jasmine decided not to push her mother any further right now. She would have to bide her time.

After breakfast, Mum gave
Holly a full health check.
She examined her all over,
took her temperature
and finally listened to
Holly's heartbeat
through her
stethoscope.

"Is she
all right?"
asked Jasmine
anxiously, when
Mum unhooked the stethoscope.

"So far as I can tell, she's absolutely fine. Clear
eyes and nose, normal temperature and a good
strong heartbeat."

"But you said her mother had probably
rejected her for a reason."

"It might be any one of a number of reasons,
though," said Mum. "We'll probably never
know. It might be something to do with the

mother, not Holly. I can't be completely certain that Holly is fully well, because there might be a problem with one of her organs that hasn't shown up yet. But she certainly seems to be a healthy little kitten. And very beautiful, too, aren't you, Holly?"

She put out her finger and Holly batted it with her tiny paw.

"She's the cutest kitten ever," said Tom. "I wish I could have her."

"Ask your mum when you get home," said Jasmine.

"I will. But she won't let me. I know she won't. She hates cats."

"She couldn't possibly hate Holly," said Jasmine. "Nobody could."

Tom went home an hour later. That afternoon, he phoned Jasmine.

"Mum saw the flea bites," he said. "She went crazy. There's no way she'll let me have Holly now."

"But Holly won't have fleas when you take her home."

"I told her that, but she wouldn't budge. It's not just the fleas. She went on and on about how cats scratch the furniture and leave hairs everywhere and bring dead animals into the house. She said cats are dirty nasty creatures and there was no way she was having one in her home. I haven't spoken to her since."

If Tom's mum was going to be so horrible about cats, Jasmine thought, then there was no way she was ever going to have Tom's mum in *her* home. How dare she call them dirty nasty creatures!

"Well," she said, "if your parents really aren't going to change their minds, I'll just have to persuade mine."

Chapter Seven
School Is
So Annoying

It was the first Monday of November, the day
school started again after half term. Mum was
stirring a pan of porridge on the big Aga stove.
Ella sat at the kitchen table with a cup of tea, a
book lying open in front of her as usual. Jasmine
was kneeling on the floor, playing with Holly.

At four weeks old, Holly was much steadier on
her feet and wonderfully playful. Jasmine pushed
a toy kitten across the tiles to her. Holly jumped
on it and started to bite it with her tiny new
teeth. Jasmine pulled the toy away and Holly

leapt on it again, nuzzling and nipping at its fur.

"It's so unfair that we have to go back to school just as Holly's getting really playful," said Jasmine. "She'll be so lonely all day without me."

Jasmine and Tom had turned Sky's puppy crate into a playpen for Holly, where she would spend the days while Jasmine was at school. The wire crate had a fleecy blanket on the floor, and contained a sleeping hammock, a box that Holly liked to hide in, and her scratching post and litter tray. Jasmine had also put some of Holly's favourite toys in there, including toilet roll tubes and ping-pong balls which she loved to chase.

"She'll be fine," Mum said. "She'll play manically for a while and then she'll curl up and sleep, and you can lavish attention on her when you get home. She'll be able to see the other cats, so she won't be lonely. And Dad's going to check on her regularly, isn't he?"

"But it's not the same as me being there," said Jasmine. "If we could bring the other kittens in when they're weaned, she'd have companions all the time."

Mum gave her a warning look. "Don't even start, Jas."

The scullery door rattled as Dad came in from the farmyard. Jasmine heard him taking off his wellington boots and washing his hands. He walked into the kitchen and warmed his hands at the Aga.

"Chilly out there," he said. "Shouldn't be surprised if we have frost tomorrow."

Mum served the porridge into bowls. Jasmine sat at the table and sprinkled hers with sugar.

Holly padded over and started batting at her trouser hems. Jasmine took a fluffy toy mouse on a string out of her pocket and dangled it in front of Holly. The kitten jumped up on her hind legs and grabbed the mouse in her front paws.

"You're so clever, aren't you?" said Jasmine, bending down to stroke her. "You're the cleverest kitten in the whole wide world."

Mum looked up as Manu walked into the kitchen, still in pyjamas.

"Oh, Manu, go and get dressed," she said. "And hurry up, or your porridge will be cold."

Manu was in the doorway when he suddenly stopped.

67

"Oops," he said.

"What?" asked Mum.

"I just remembered. I have to go to school dressed as Samuel Pepys."

"*What?*" said Mum and Dad together.

"Yes, we're doing the Great Fire of London and I'm Samuel Pepys."

"But that's ridiculous," said Mum. "We'd have had a letter if you had to dress up today. They'd have given us some warning, at least."

Manu looked sheepish. "There might have been a letter."

"Where is it?" asked Mum in her deadliest voice.

Manu took his book bag from one of the coat pegs on the wall, rummaged amongst its contents and eventually produced a crumpled paper aeroplane.

He handed it to Mum. She unfolded it, read the letter and sat down heavily.

"Oh, dear lord, the local paper's coming in to photograph the whole of Year One in their 1666 costumes this morning. Manu, how could you have forgotten to mention this for the entire two-week holiday?"

"He'll just have to go in a bin liner," said Dad. "I'm sure Samuel Pepys wore something black and shiny."

"He can't go in a bin liner again," said Mum. "You'll have to do something, Michael. I need to be at the surgery in half an hour."

"I'd love to," said Dad, "but I've got a bloke coming to deliver the new calf feeders, remember?"

The doorbell rang. "That'll be him," said Dad. "Sorry, must be off." He practically sprinted out of the door.

Mum put her head in her hands. "I can't believe you've landed me in this, Manu. What on earth am I going to do?"

"I'll make him a costume," said Ella.

They all stared at Ella. She held out her phone, on which was a picture of an old-fashioned man in a long curly wig and a shirt with ruffles under a brown jacket.

"That's him," said Manu excitedly. "That's Samuel Pepys!"

"I'll need your black leggings, Jas," said Ella, "and your white knee-length socks to go over them. I'll make some buckles out of foil for Manu's shoes."

"But you'll be late for school," said Mum.

"I'll only miss registration," said Ella. "It'll be fine."

Jasmine was studying the picture. "He can wear his normal school shirt," she said, "and we can tear up some strips of sheet from the rag bag to be the ruffles."

"If we put a belt round Mum's brown jacket," said Ella, "that will be perfect."

"And he can have that wig from the dressing up box," said Jasmine. "I'll cut it and brush it a bit."

Mum was staring at her daughters in wonder. "You're angels, you really are. I'm eternally grateful to you. Just remember to put Holly in her playpen before you leave, won't you, Jas?"

Jasmine picked Holly up. "Look at her beautiful little face," she said to Mum. "She hasn't been any trouble, has she?"

"She's been very good," said Mum. "Where are my car keys?"

Jasmine fetched them from the dresser. "And she gets on fine with the other cats, doesn't she?"

"Thanks," said Mum, taking the keys. "Yes, they seem to have settled down well together."

"So it wouldn't be any trouble to keep her, would it?"

Jasmine fixed her mother with what she hoped was a soulful gaze.

"An extra animal always means more work," said Mum. "Not to mention more expense."

"But she's so lovely," said Jasmine. "Who would want to get rid of such a beautiful little kitten? You don't really want to let her go, do you?"

Mum sighed. "Jasmine, you promised not to pester. And this really isn't the time to discuss it. I have to go to work, and you have to make a costume and go to school."

Jasmine sighed. "School is so annoying. Six whole hours in the same room as Bella Bradley. Ugh."

Jasmine and Manu arrived at school just as
everyone was filing into the building. Manu,
resplendent in wig and ruffles, made his way to
the Infants. Jasmine's classmates were hanging up
their coats outside their classroom. There was lots
of chatting going on, but Bella Bradley's voice
could be heard above everybody else's.

"What are you getting for Christmas?" she
asked her friend Sadie. "My parents said I could
get a new pet."

"You're so lucky," sighed Sadie. "You've already
got a dog."

"Rupert's not all mine, though," said Bella.
"He belongs to the whole family."

Jasmine and Tom exchanged glances. Bella's
dog Rupert had killed Button's mother as she
had sat on her nest last spring. Bella had been
letting him run free amongst Jasmine's dad's
sheep.

"I can't choose between a puppy and a kitten,"
said Bella. "I've been researching, and I've seen

73

the cutest little cat collars and cat beds, and these gorgeous matching feeding bowls."

"Why don't you get a kitten then?" asked Sadie.

"Yes, but then if I get a puppy, you can buy the most amazing coats for them, and if you get one of those tiny ones you can carry it around in a special puppy handbag. I wish I could get both. It's not fair."

"Ugh," said Jasmine to Tom, as they walked into the classroom. "I can't believe she's getting a pet and all she cares about is what accessories she can buy for it."

"She shouldn't even be allowed to have a pet," said Tom, "after letting her dog kill Button's mother."

"If I ever meet her parents," said Jasmine, "I'll tell them how irresponsible they are."

"I don't suppose your mum has changed her mind about you bringing the other kittens indoors?" said Tom.

"Nope. Has your mum changed her mind about you having Holly?"

"No," said Tom gloomily. "I've tried and tried, but she won't budge."

"Why are our parents so unreasonable?" said Jasmine. "We've already got cats, so a couple more kittens in our house just for a few weeks wouldn't make any difference. I bet they wouldn't even notice them. And your mum works from home, so you'd think she'd be happy to have a beautiful little kitten to keep her company."

"I know," said Tom. "I don't understand them at all."

Chapter Eight
This Is
Our Chance

"Do you like it?" Jasmine asked Tom. "We put the tree up earlier than usual, because of this dinner party."

"It looks amazing," said Tom. "Your decorations are so nice."

Jasmine turned to the kitten in her arms. "Isn't it pretty, Holly?"

"She loves the lights," said Tom. "Look how she's staring at them."

It was four weeks later, and Holly was eight weeks old. Mum and Dad were giving a dinner party tonight. Jasmine couldn't remember them ever doing such a thing before, but Mum had decided that they owed several people an invitation and they might as well invite them all at once and get it over with. Although it was still only morning, Mum had already laid the dining table with candles and wine glasses and the antique china that had belonged to Jasmine's grandmother.

"And I know we usually wait until Christmas Eve to decorate the tree," she had said, "but it will be nice to have the house looking festive. And if the tree's up, hopefully everyone will look at that and not the dust."

So they had fetched a tree from the woods yesterday afternoon, and had spent this morning decorating it. Holly had been banished from the room after causing havoc by leaping into boxes of decorations, shredding tissue paper and manically chasing baubles around the floor.

While the dinner party was going on, the children were also to be banished, in their case to the sitting room for pizza and TV, which to Jasmine seemed by far the better option.

"Don't let the cats anywhere near this room from now on, will you?" said Mum, adjusting a tablemat by half a centimetre.

"I won't," said Jasmine. "We just brought Holly down to see the fairy lights."

"Well, pop her back in her playpen and go and fetch the cat basket for those kittens."

As the kittens were now weaned, Mum had decided it was time to trap, neuter and return them and their mother to the shed, before the cat became pregnant again. Despite all Jasmine's attempts at persuasion, she had remained firm.

"They'll be perfectly happy in the shed," she said. "You can still put food out for them.

They'll have a good life as farm cats and they'll help to keep the vermin down."

Over the past few weeks, Jasmine had gradually moved the cat's food and water bowls closer and closer to the tool shed, until finally she had put them in the shed itself. She had also put a cardboard box lined with an old blanket in there, so they didn't have to sleep on sacks.

Jasmine had hoped that the cat would become friendly if she was being fed, and then she would be able to play with the kittens and tame them. But it hadn't worked out that way. The cat tolerated Jasmine bringing food in, but she hissed and spat if she tried to approach her kittens.

So Jasmine just watched them through the shed window, as they jumped on to boxes, scrabbled over sacks, tumbled in and out of plant pots and endlessly wrestled each other, rolling over and over on the dusty floor, nipping each other's tails and fur. They tried to play with their mother, too, but she mostly just batted them away with her paw.

"I bet it would only take us a few days to tame them," said Jasmine now, as they walked to the shed with the cat basket. "We could probably have them tamed by Monday if you'd let us bring them indoors."

Mum pretended she hadn't heard.

The trap for the mother cat was a large cage with a spring door that could be set to snap shut when the cat stepped on a metal plate on the cage floor. It had already been in the shed for a few days, with the spring door wedged open. Jasmine had put the food bowl inside it, so the cat had got used to walking into the trap for her food. Last night, Mum had set the spring once Jasmine had placed the food bowl inside, and the cat had walked into the trap straightaway. She hissed and spat at first, but they had put a blanket over the trap to make her feel safe, and she had calmed down after a while.

"I know it doesn't seem nice to trap her," Mum had said, "but she'll be much happier and healthier in the long run. And we have to catch her the night before, because she'll only walk into the trap for food, and she can't have any food for twelve hours before the operation."

They had blocked up the hole in the shed wall

so the kittens couldn't escape, and Jasmine had removed their food bowl before she went to bed, so that they too would have empty stomachs before their operations.

Now, Mum softly opened the door. The cat was sleeping in the trap and the kittens were curled up in their box.

Tom and Jasmine, each holding a small towel, crept towards the sleeping kittens. They caught each other's eyes and then, at exactly the same time, they each picked up a kitten, wrapped it snugly in a towel and held it close to their chests.

"Neatly done, you two," said Mum. "Good work."

Jasmine smiled at the beautiful tabby kitten in her arms. It had blue eyes and thick fluffy fur. It was miaowing but not struggling. She held it against her chest and stroked it gently from behind, up the forehead and down between the ears. "Hello, little one," she said.

The ginger kitten was wilder than the tabby. It

was struggling, hissing and spitting. Tom held it firmly and stroked the back of its head.

"Look at its eyes," he said. "They're bright green."

"They're amazing," said Jasmine. "Are they boys or girls, Mum?"

Mum took the tabby kitten and examined it. "This one's a girl."

Tom handed her the ginger kitten. She held it in the towel as she examined it. "And this one's a boy."

The kitten stopped struggling and fixed his big green eyes on Mum. She looked back at it. "You are very lovely," she said.

Tom and Jasmine glanced at each other. Was Mum weakening?

Mum handed the kitten back to Tom. "Right, pop them in the basket and drape the towels on top."

Her phone rang and she stepped into the garden to answer it. She was on call again this weekend.

With a heavy heart, Jasmine placed the tabby kitten in the plastic cat carrier. Tom did the same with her brother. The kittens miaowed and ran to the sides, trying to escape from this strange new prison.

"It's OK," said Jasmine. "You're all safe. And you won't be in there for long."

Mum came back into the shed. "Bad timing, I'm afraid. I've got to go to a calving. I shouldn't be long. Just put the kittens' basket next to the trap, and I'll take them to the surgery when I get back. Give them a bowl of water and they'll be fine for an hour or two. Thank goodness Dad's cooking tonight. I'll see you soon."

She hurried off.

Jasmine looked at Tom, her eyes gleaming with excitement.

"This is our chance! I bet we could tame them in a couple of hours. Let's take them inside."

Tom's eyes lit up. Then they clouded over with doubt. "What about your mum?"

Jasmine shrugged. "What can she do? She can only put them outdoors again, and she's doing that already. And this way, we've got one more chance to convince her that we can look after all three of them. Come on. Let's see if these two remember their sister."

In Jasmine's room, Holly was dribbling a ping

pong ball around her playpen. She stopped and ran to the side of the pen when Tom and Jasmine came in. They set the basket gently on the floor next to her.

"Holly, your sister and brother are in this basket," said Jasmine. "Do you remember them?"

"Holly must smell completely different now," said Tom. "They won't recognise her scent."

He lifted the towels off the cat basket. The kittens ran at the sides, trying to find a way out. Tom and Jasmine spoke to them softly, trying to calm them down. Holly shrank back and watched her sister and brother intently from a safe distance.

"They'll be exhausted in a minute," said Jasmine.

Sure enough, after a few minutes the kittens started to calm down. "We should pick them up and handle them," said Tom.

"We need to pick Holly up too," said Jasmine, "or she'll get jealous. I'll fetch Ella."

87

Ella was quite happy to be called away from her books to come and pet a kitten. "You take the tabby," said Jasmine. "She's tamer. I'll take the wild one and Tom can pet Holly. Ella, you take the lid off the basket and Tom and I will get the kittens."

They wrapped the kittens in towels and Tom handed the tabby to Ella while he let Holly out of her playpen. Holly purred as he held her and talked to her. The other two kittens struggled and mewed as Jasmine and Ella stroked them.

"You should call the ginger kitten Mistletoe," said Ella, "because his eyes are the colour of mistletoe leaves."

"Then the tabby should be Ivy," said Tom.

"Holly, Ivy and Mistletoe," said Jasmine. "Perfect."

She turned as the door opened. Ben and Manu stood in the doorway. Their eyes lit up as they saw the kittens.

"You brought them in!" said Manu. "Did Mum change her mind?"

"Not exactly," said Jasmine, "but we're going to tame them and then she will."

"We should do that experiment on them," Ben said to Manu.

"Oh, yes," said Manu. "Can we borrow one, Jas?"

Jasmine held Mistletoe closer. "No way are you two coming near these kittens," she said. "What experiment, anyway?"

"It's a science experiment we thought up," said

Ben. "You know how everyone says cats always land on their feet?"

"And everyone says toast always lands butter side down," said Manu. "So we thought, if we tied a piece of buttered toast to a cat's back and dropped it out of a window, we could see which way up it landed, and then we'd know which rule was stronger."

"If you dare come anywhere near these kittens, Manu," said Jasmine, "I'll tie a piece of toast to your back and throw you out of a window. Then you can see how you like it."

Chapter Nine

What Have You Done With Them?

It wasn't long before all three kittens were fast asleep. Ella brought her homework into Jasmine's room, so she could guard them from kidnap attempts while Jasmine and Tom took Sky for a walk.

Mum still wasn't back when they returned. Ella was sitting at Jasmine's desk, surrounded by books, typing on her laptop. But the doors of the basket and the playpen were wide open, and the kittens were nowhere to be seen.

"Ella," said Jasmine, "where are the kittens?"

"What?" said Ella vaguely, her eyes on the screen.

"Where did you put the kittens?"

"Nowhere. Why?"

"Oh no," said Tom. "Manu and Ben must have sneaked in and taken them."

Jasmine's face blazed with fury. "I'll kill them!"

Manu's room was empty. Tom and Jasmine raced downstairs. Manu and Ben were sitting on the living-room sofa, watching cartoons.

"Where are the kittens?" said Jasmine, looking wildly around the room. "Where are they?"

The boys remained glued to the TV. Jasmine grabbed the remote and switched it off. Ben and Manu swung their heads round, their faces the picture of outrage.

"Hey!" shouted Manu. "What are you doing?"

"What have you done with the kittens?" yelled Jasmine.

"They're here somewhere. We were playing with them. Give me the remote."

"But they're not here, are they? What have you done with them?"

"We didn't do anything. They must have gone somewhere else."

"You idiots!" yelled Jasmine. "They're only eight weeks old. Anything could have happened to them!"

Tom was running around the room, lifting up cushions and looking under furniture. Then he turned to Jasmine, looking panic-stricken.

"What if they've gone in the dining room?" he said.

Jasmine stared at him for a second. Then they ran into the hall. The dining room door stood ajar. They pushed it open.

The first thing they saw was Holly and Mistletoe, chasing each other around the dining table. As Jasmine ran to grab them, Holly's tail swiped the stem of a wine glass. It crashed against a candlestick and smashed into tiny pieces. Holly leapt off the table in fright and landed on Marmite, who was dozing on the carpet.

Marmite sprang up in alarm and tried to jump on to the table, but she misjudged the distance and ended up clinging to the edge of the white tablecloth with her claws. The cloth started slipping off the table, pulling glasses, tablemats and candlesticks with it, as Marmite struggled desperately to disentangle her claws from the fabric.

As Tom dashed over to free her, a wine glass rolled off the table and crashed to the floor. Marmite jerked back in shock, finally freed herself and sprang up into the Christmas tree. It wobbled and shook. Toffee jumped into the tree

94

after her. They chased
each other around the
branches, sending baubles
and decorations crashing
to the floor. Jasmine
and Tom tried to
grab them, but they
climbed up out of
 reach.

　　Then Jasmine
spotted Mistletoe, perched
on the very top branch. As
Marmite ran towards him,
Mistletoe leapt from the
tree to the bookcase,
sending all the Christmas
cards toppling to the carpet.
Meanwhile, Holly had discovered a
roll of wrapping paper at the side of the
room. Pushing at the tube, she managed in
a few seconds to unroll the entire three metres.

Ivy leapt on the end of the paper as it curled up,
biting it and tearing it with her claws.

Toffee and Marmite were both at the top of
the tree now. Marmite hissed at Toffee and lashed
out with her paw. Jasmine and Tom looked on
in helpless horror as Toffee sprang out of the
tree and landed on the dresser, knocking over
Mum's vase of flowers. The water spilled on to
Holly and Ivy and soaked their roll of wrapping
paper. The drenched kittens howled in shock and
started running madly around the room. Toffee
shot out into the hall.

The door from the kitchen opened and Dad appeared, holding a bunch of carrots.

"What on *earth* is going on?" he shouted.

Spooked by the shouting, Marmite leapt from the topmost branch of the tree. At least, she tried to leap, but her paws got caught in the lights and the force of her attempt unbalanced the whole thing. The tree came crashing down on the dining table,

smashing the remaining wine glasses and
scattering pine needles and decorations all over
the room. Marmite disentangled herself with
a yowl of terror and fled. All three kittens shot
from the room in different directions.

A terrible silence descended on the dining
room. The only sound was the drip, drip, drip of
water from the overturned vase. Jasmine didn't
dare look at her father.

The key turned in the front door. Mum's car
keys clattered on to the hall table. Mum appeared
in the dining room doorway and her eyes
widened in horror.

"What have you done?" she shrieked. "Jasmine
Green, what *have* you done?"

When Jasmine confessed that she had brought
the kittens in, her parents were angrier than she
had ever seen them. They sent Tom off to find
the kittens, and then they rounded on her.

"This is *exactly* why we told you not to bring

those kittens indoors," said Dad. "You were told again and again, and you completely disobeyed us."

"We were going to tame them," said Jasmine. "It was all Manu's fault. He let them out. We were being responsible."

"Responsible!" shouted Mum. "Responsible? What you did, Jasmine, is the exact opposite of responsible."

"But—" Jasmine began.

"Don't you dare argue back," said Mum. "Look at the state of this place. Every one of those breakages is coming out of yours and Manu's pocket money. And I was going to clean the bathroom after I'd operated on the cats, and now I'm going to have to clean up this room instead. So you are going to clean the bathroom, and the downstairs toilet, and they had better be sparkling clean or you'll do them again."

"And then you can peel all the vegetables for dinner," said Dad, "because I won't have time to do it now. And those two boys can switch off that television and fill up the log baskets. There'll be no more television for any of you today. I've got enough jobs to keep you all busy until you go to bed at six o'clock."

"Six o'clock!" said Jasmine.

"You heard me," said Dad.

"And in the morning," said Mum, "you can write out an advertisement for Holly and we'll find her a proper home."

"No!" said Jasmine. "Please, Mum…"

"I won't hear another word about it," said Mum. "If you're not responsible enough to listen to instructions, you're certainly not responsible enough to have another cat. We're advertising Holly tomorrow."

Chapter Ten

You Can't Let Her Go There

The first people who phoned about the advertisement arranged to come and see Holly on Wednesday evening. Two more families were coming on Thursday.

Ivy and Mistletoe were back in the shed with their mother. In her heart of hearts, Jasmine had to admit they seemed happier outdoors. And they had all been neutered now, so they should have healthy lives.

But Holly wasn't a feral kitten any more. She was tame and socialised, and she needed a home.

When the doorbell rang as the family was finishing dinner on Tuesday, Mum clapped her hand to her mouth. "Oh, blast, it's those people. I completely forgot."

"What people?" asked Jasmine.

"I bumped into one of the mums from your school this morning, and she said her daughter really wanted a kitten, and could I recommend any breeders. So I said why didn't she come and look at Holly."

Jasmine stared at her mother in alarm. "What was her name?"

"Tina," said Mum, walking to the door. "I think her daughter's in your class."

Jasmine jumped up from her chair. "Mum, you can't! She's—"

But Mum was already in the hall. "Jasmine!" she called. "Go and fetch Holly."

Jasmine stomped upstairs. "Don't worry," she whispered to Holly, as she scooped her out of the playpen. "There's no way I'm letting you go to her."

When Jasmine brought Holly into the living room, Bella Bradley and her mum were sitting on the sofa opposite Nadia. Bella, who had never spoken nicely to Jasmine in her life, now greeted her as if they were best friends. Then, as her eyes fell on Holly, she opened them very wide and said, "Oh, she's so cute!"

She turned to Nadia with a simpering smile. "Could I possibly hold her, Mrs Green?"

Seething inside, Jasmine handed Holly over.

"Oh, thank you, Jasmine," Bella said sweetly. "Look, Mummy, isn't she the cutest little kitty you ever saw?"

She started talking to Holly in a sickly voice, the kind some people use when talking to babies. Her mother smiled at her fondly.

"Bella adores animals," she said proudly to Jasmine's mum. "She's been so wanting one of her own. And she's an only child, so it's nice for her to have pets, isn't it?"

103

"Do you have other animals?" asked Mum.

"Just a dog," said Tina, "and he's as good as gold. He won't be any problem with a kitten."

"Is that the dog who killed a nesting duck in my dad's sheep field?" asked Jasmine, trying to keep her voice calm. "Didn't the police come round to your house afterwards?"

Tina went red. Bella looked up at Nadia with big sad eyes.

"That was so, so terrible," she said. "I cried for days about that poor duck, didn't I, Mummy?"

Jasmine opened her mouth to remind Bella that her exact words when she had seen the dead mallard were, "So? It's just a duck." But before she could speak, Bella hurried on.

"I think I was in shock at the time, because it was so awful, but I cried for days afterwards, didn't I, Mummy? And it really taught me a lesson. I've never taken Rupert out without a lead since then. And if I see anyone else in a sheep field with a loose dog, I always tell them to put it on a lead. So I might have actually saved the life of other innocent animals. It would be nice to think I've done something to make up for that terrible day. I'm so, so sorry, Mrs Green. I still feel really bad about it. And Jasmine was so amazing to save the little duckling, wasn't she?"

Jasmine glanced at Mum. Surely she wasn't going to fall for this?

"Well, that's very nice of you to say," said Mum. "Anyone can make a mistake, and it's great that you've learned from it."

"Thank you, Mrs Green. That's so kind of you. Oh, listen, Mummy, she's purring! I think she likes me."

"Of course she does, darling," said Tina. "She's such a cute little thing, isn't she?"

Jasmine looked sadly at Holly. Even she had fallen for Bella's act.

"Would you like her, do you think, sweetie?" asked Tina.

"Oh, yes, please, Mummy. I'd like her more than anything. She's the cutest kitten ever."

Jasmine couldn't bear this. She had to have one last try at saving Holly.

"There is one thing we need to tell you," she said.

"Yes?" said Tina.

"The thing is," Jasmine said, "Holly was rejected by her mother. And that might mean there's something wrong with her. Cats usually reject their kittens for a reason, so even though she seems all right at the moment, there may be a problem with one of her internal organs that hasn't shown up yet."

Tina looked alarmed. Nadia laughed.

"Oh, honestly, Jasmine," she said. "That's nonsense and you know it."

"You said it yourself! You said there might be something wrong with her that we don't know about yet. And it wouldn't be fair to sell Bella a kitten that isn't healthy."

"I said that when she was two weeks old," said Mum. "She's over eight weeks old now and I've never seen a healthier kitten."

"We'll definitely take her, then," said Tina. "We'll collect her next week."

Bella threw her arms around her mother's neck. "Oh, thank you, thank you so much, Mummy! You're the loveliest, kindest mummy in the whole wide world."

Jasmine made a noise as though she was about to be sick. Mum shot her a furious look.

As they were leaving, Bella glanced at Jasmine and said, "I don't really like the name Holly. I think I'm going to give her another name. Would that be all right, Mrs Green?"

"Of course," said Mum. "You can call her anything you like, once she's your kitten."

"No," said Jasmine, once Mum had shut the front door. "Just no. I'm not letting Holly go to Bella Bradley."

Mum held up her palms. "I'm not listening, Jasmine. Holly is going and that is that."

"But her dog's a duck murderer! What if he kills Holly? He easily could. She's way smaller than a duck. You can't let her go there, Mum, you just can't."

"Honestly, Jasmine," said Mum, "I've absolutely had enough of your pestering. Those people seemed perfectly nice, and dogs and cats live together quite happily in millions of households."

"But she doesn't even want a kitten! She just wants all the cute accessories. We heard her talking about it at school. She'll get bored with Holly after a few weeks. She won't love her properly. Not like I do."

Mum looked as though she was about to explode.

"OK, OK," said Jasmine. "I know I'm not allowed to keep her. But can't we wait until the other people have been to look at her and then see who'd be the best owner?"

Mum took a deep breath.

"The truth is, Jasmine," she said, in the quiet, deadly voice that Jasmine hated, "you don't want Holly to go to anyone. You've been determined to keep her ever since you first brought her in. The most perfect family in the world could walk through that door right now and you'd find some reason why they weren't right. Bella might be a bit sickly sweet, but she clearly liked Holly and I'm sure she'll look after her."

Jasmine opened her mouth again.

"That's enough, Jasmine," said her mother. "I mean it. Holly has found a new home and I don't want to hear another word from you."

Chapter Eleven
A Bit of a Shock

Tom came to the farm on the following Sunday to play with Holly for the last time. Bella was going to collect her the next day.

"I brought her some new toys," he said, pulling from his rucksack a knitted Father Christmas and two silver baubles. "The baubles aren't glass, so they won't smash. She can take them to her new home, to remind her of us."

Holly loved her new toys, and spent a happy hour chasing the baubles and wrestling with Father Christmas.

"I bet Bella won't play with her for long," said Tom.

"No, she'll get bored after a few days, like she does with everything," said Jasmine.

"And then Holly will be really lonely," said Tom.

Jasmine glanced at him. He looked sadder than she had ever seen him.

"Maybe she'll be OK," she said, not because she believed it, but to try to make Tom feel better. "Some cats like to be left alone."

Tom shook his head. "Not Holly. She likes company."

After lunch, they played with Holly until she curled up and fell asleep on Jasmine's jumper. Jasmine put her in her playpen while she and Tom took Sky for a walk and went to see Truffle. When they returned, Tom went upstairs to check on Holly, while Jasmine groomed Sky in the scullery.

The phone rang while Jasmine was washing Sky's food bowl. A couple of minutes later, Mum came out to the scullery, the phone in her hand. She looked furious.

"That is unbelievable," she said. "What a cheek. Complete waste of time."

"What?" said Jasmine.

"Those Bradleys."

"Oh, them," said Jasmine scornfully. "What have they done now?"

"I hate to admit it," said Mum, "but you were right about Bella Bradley all along."

"Of course I was," said Jasmine. "Why, what's happened?"

"That was Tina on the phone. They're not going to take Holly any more."

Jasmine stared at her. "No way. Really?"

"Really. They've changed their minds."

Jasmine whooped in delight. "Oh, that's amazing! Why did they change their minds?"

"Apparently Bella decided she didn't want a

kitten after all. She wants a new phone instead."

Jasmine snorted. "See? I told you what she's like."

Mum sighed. "I know. I should have listened to you. It made me very thankful that you really care about your animals."

Jasmine looked disgusted. "As if I'd ever be like Bella Bradley."

"It's such a nuisance, though," said Mum. "I rang the other people who'd enquired about Holly, but they've all found other kittens now, and it's too close to Christmas to re-advertise. We'll have to wait until after New Year."

"Unless…" said Jasmine, giving her mother what she hoped was an irresistibly appealing look.

"Unless what?"

"Well, you did say how good I am at looking after animals. And Holly's so cute and beautiful. You wouldn't really want her to go to another home, would you? You'd miss her too, I know

113

you would."

Mum hesitated. "Well…"

"Please, Mum? Please? For my Christmas present? I'd never get bored with her, you know I wouldn't."

"Well," said Mum, "you have looked after her very well, and she is lovely."

Jasmine held her breath.

Mum smiled. "All right then, Jasmine. Holly can be your Christmas present."

Jasmine gasped in delight and threw her arms around her mother. "Oh, thank you, Mum! Thank you so, so much! I'm going to tell Tom. And I'm going to tell Holly she can stay with me forever. Thank you *so* much, Mum."

She ran into the hall. "Tom!" she called. "Come down here! I've got the best news!"

The doorbell rang. Jasmine opened the door. Tom's mum was standing on the step.

"Hello, Mel," said Mum, coming into the hall. "Come in."

"I won't, thank you," said Mel. "I'm afraid I need to take Tom home."

Tom appeared on the stairs, with Holly in his arms. "You said I was staying for tea," he said to Mel. "Why are you so early?"

"Are you all right?" Mum asked her. "You don't look well."

Mel's face contorted, as though she was trying not to cry. "It's just … we've had a bit of a shock." She swallowed. "It's Richard's mother. Tom's granny."

"What?" said Tom, hurrying to the door. "What's happened?"

"Oh, Tom," said Mel, bending down and putting her hands on his shoulders. "Tom, I'm so sorry. Granny has died."

Chapter Twelve
An Answer
For Everything

Tom came to school as normal during the last week of term, but he was not at all like his usual self. He looked really sad all the time and he barely spoke a word. During lessons he seemed very far away, and Jasmine could tell he didn't hear anything the teacher said. When they were meant to be working, Tom just sat with a pencil in his hand, staring into space.

The worst thing, Jasmine thought, was that the rest of the class was in a state of feverish excitement. Every afternoon was spent making decorations for the classroom, or Christmas cards for their parents, or practising for the Christmas show. Tom joined in all these activities, but Jasmine could tell how sad he was inside, and her heart ached for her friend. It was going to be such a lonely Christmas for him.

On the last day of term, Tom came to the farm for tea. He was going to Cornwall the next day for the funeral, and he wouldn't be back until Christmas Eve. He and Jasmine took Sky for a walk, fed Truffle and then played with Holly in Jasmine's room.

"I'm so glad you got to keep her," Tom said. "I couldn't have stood it if Bella had taken her. I would have worried about her all the time."

"Jasmine," called Mum up the stairs, "there's juice and biscuits if you want some."

"I'll come and get it," Jasmine called back.

In the kitchen, Tom's mum was talking to Nadia. She looked tired and stressed. Jasmine put the juice and biscuits on a tray and was heading out of the room when Mel said, "Jasmine, before you go… How does Tom seem to you?"

"Er…" said Jasmine, a little thrown by the question. "Well, he seems sad."

"I wondered if he'd said anything in particular to you. I'm worried about him. He's so unhappy all the time."

"It is very recent," said Mum. "It will take time."

"I know," said Mel, "and I know he's going to be sad for a long time. He loved his granny very much. It's just… It feels like it's more than that, somehow. I've always worried about him being lonely, as an only child, but he's never seemed particularly lonely before. But now… Well, this week, he seems incredibly lonely. And Christmas is going to be so hard for him. He was so looking forward to going to Cornwall, and now it will just be the three of us at home together."

"Why don't you come to us for Christmas?" asked Mum. "We'd love to have you."

 119

"That's so kind," said Mel, "but I think Richard wants to be at home. I'm just worried about Tom."

"Well, you know he can come here whenever he likes," said Mum. "He's always welcome."

A peal of laughter sounded from upstairs. Mel looked startled.

"Was that Tom?" she said. "Who's he with? I haven't heard him laugh all week."

Suddenly, a strange sensation ran through Jasmine. It was unlike anything she had ever felt before: a curious mixture of excitement, pain and hope. But despite the confusion of feelings, in that moment Jasmine knew, with absolute clarity, what it was she had to do.

She put the tray back on the table. "Come

A Kitten Called Holly

up and see him," she said to Mel. "But be really quiet."

Looking a bit bemused, Mel followed her up the stairs. Jasmine stopped outside the open door of her bedroom and stepped aside so that Mel had a clear view.

Tom was sprawled on the carpet with his back to them. He had attached a long piece of string to each of the baubles, and he was pulling them across the carpet in little jerky movements, first one and then the other. Holly was darting between them, pouncing on each in turn as it moved.

Tom let go of the strings and threw the Father Christmas toy high in the air. Holly leapt up to grab it, but missed and turned a complete back somersault before landing on her feet. Tom laughed and scooped her into his arms. "You're the best kitten ever," he said.

As he cuddled her, his face became sad again. Mel put her hand on Jasmine's arm and gestured for her to come downstairs.

She didn't speak until they were in the kitchen. Then she said, "It's funny. I've never been an animal person myself, but Tom really does love animals, doesn't he?"

Mum handed her a mug of tea, which she accepted gratefully. "I almost wish now," Mel said, "that I'd let him have that kitten. But I really don't like cats, what with the scratching and the fleas and the hair they leave everywhere and the dead things they bring in. I just don't know if I could have one in the house."

"Holly only had fleas when we first found her," said Jasmine. "She's really clean now. And we've trained her to use her scratching post instead of furniture. If you groom her regularly

122

she won't shed much hair, and you can get her a collar with a bell, so she won't be able to catch mice and birds."

Mel smiled at her. "You have an answer for everything, don't you? But aren't you keeping Holly yourself?"

"I was going to," said Jasmine. "But Tom loves her just as much as I do, and he needs her more. It would make him really happy, I know it would."

"What do you think, Nadia?" asked Mel.

"Well," said Nadia, "I think Jasmine might be right, actually. Tom really loves Holly, and she seems to love him, too. She might be just what he needs."

Mel sat silently with her elbows on the table, cradling her mug. Eventually she said, "Let me have a think. I'll talk to Richard tonight. And please, don't say a word to Tom."

Chapter Thirteen
Happy Christmas, Tom

It was Christmas Eve. Jasmine placed Holly's
cat basket on the back seat of Mum's car and
climbed in next to it. She was holding a big
shoebox, empty except for Holly's blanket
and her woolly Father Christmas. Jasmine
had covered the box and lid with Christmas
wrapping paper, and made some small holes in
the sides.

Jasmine hadn't seen Tom since Sunday,
although she had spoken to him on the phone
from Cornwall. She had also had one very

important phone conversation with his mum.
Mel knew that Jasmine was coming to their
house this morning, but Tom had no idea.

As they drove up the farm track, an icy white
flake landed on the windscreen.

"Look!" said Jasmine. "It's snowing!"

More snowflakes splatted against the glass. "It's
properly snowing!" said Jasmine, in delight. "It's
going to be a white Christmas!"

"We'll see," said Mum. "It might not settle."

But by the time they arrived at Tom's house,
the fields and gardens already looked as though
they had been sprinkled with icing sugar.

"It *is* settling," said Jasmine. "You're going to
see snow for the first time, Holly. You're going to
have a white Christmas."

She opened the cat basket, lifted out the little
kitten and kissed the top of her head. "You're
not mine any more," she whispered, "but I'll still
see you all the time. And you're going to have a
lovely home."

She placed Holly in the shoebox and put the lid on. "It's only for a minute," she reassured her. "You'll be coming out of there very soon."

Mum ruffled Jasmine's hair. "I'm very proud of you, Jas. You're doing a good thing."

"I know," said Jasmine. She walked up the garden path with the box in her arms and rang the bell.

Inside the house, Mel called, "Tom! Someone's come to see you."

Tom's footsteps sounded on the stairs. "Who is it?"

"Why don't you open the door and see?"

Tom opened the door. His face lit up. "Hi, Jasmine! I didn't know you were coming."

"I wanted to surprise you," said Jasmine.

"Come in, both of you," said Mel.

She led them into the living room, where Tom's dad was putting lights on a Christmas tree.

"We're a bit late with everything this year," he said. "I was hoping you and Tom might decorate the tree, Jasmine, once I've done the lights."

"I'd love to," said Jasmine.

Mum started asking Tom's dad about the funeral and saying how sorry she was, but Mel interrupted. "Shall we let Jasmine give Tom his Christmas present first? Then we can go to the kitchen and I'll make us some tea."

Jasmine's stomach fluttered as she handed the

box to Tom. Standing in front of him, all her sadness about giving Holly away disappeared. She felt only excitement as she thought how happy Tom was going to be.

"Happy Christmas, Tom," she said. "I hope you like it."

"Thank you," said Tom, as he took the box. He gave it a little shake.

"Don't do that," said Jasmine in alarm. "It's fragile."

"Fragile?" He looked at Jasmine suspiciously. "It's not a mouse skeleton, is it?"

Jasmine laughed. She and Tom had put the mouse skeleton they had found in the shed into a shoebox and wrapped it up to give to Manu for Christmas.

"Open it and see," she said. "It's not taped up."

Tom set the box on the floor and knelt beside it. He took off the lid. Holly looked up at him and gave a loud miaow.

Tom's mouth fell open. He looked up at

128

Jasmine, and then at his parents, with huge
amazed eyes.

Then he said, "Holly? But … she's yours. Are
you lending her to me?"

Jasmine shook her head. "She's yours now. I
wanted to give her to you and your mum said I
could."

Tom seemed to have lost the power of speech.
He stared at Jasmine, then at his parents, then at
Holly, then at his parents again.

Eventually he said, in a dazed voice, "Really? Is
it true? Is she really mine?"

Jasmine was smiling so hard she couldn't speak: she could only nod. Tom's mum said, "It's true. She's really yours, Tom."

Tom let out a cry of delight. He scooped Holly out of the box and held her to his chest. "Oh, thank you, thank you, thank you!" he said, stroking Holly and staring in amazement at Jasmine and his parents. "Thank you so, so much! I can't believe it."

He cuddled Holly to his chest and she purred loudly. Tom looked up again, his face still amazed.

"She's really mine?" he asked again. "To keep?"

"She's really yours," said his mum. "She's yours to keep. For ever."

As Jasmine walked home that afternoon, she didn't even need the snow to make her feel Christmassy. For the first time in her life, she felt she understood the saying that it is better to give than to receive. No present she received that Christmas could possibly bring her as much pleasure as the happiness she had felt when she had given Holly to Tom.

When she opened her bedroom door, though, and saw the empty space where Holly's playpen had been, she suddenly felt very sad. Holly was gone, and there wouldn't be any more kittens now.

Dad came into the room and put his arm around her.

"Feeling sad?" he asked.

"A bit," said Jasmine.

He squeezed her shoulder. "You did a good thing, Jasmine. You saved Holly's life and she's gone to a fantastic home. You should be very proud of yourself."

"And I've still got Toffee and Marmite," said Jasmine. "And Button and Truffle and Sky."

"Exactly," said Dad. "And I've been thinking. Sky is just the right age to start proper sheepdog training now. What do you say to rigging up a pen and starting him on some herding practice?

131

We could begin on Boxing Day."

"Oh, yes, please!" said Jasmine. "That would be perfect."

As Jasmine was about to hang up her stocking that evening, the phone rang. It was Tom.

"She's sleeping in her playpen next to my bed," he said. "I still can't believe she's really mine. I can't believe she'll still be there when I wake up in the morning."

"I'm so glad you can keep her," said Jasmine. "She's going to love living with you."

"Mum said it was you who persuaded her," said Tom. "She said it was all down to you. Thank you so, so much, Jasmine. Holly is the best present I've ever had."

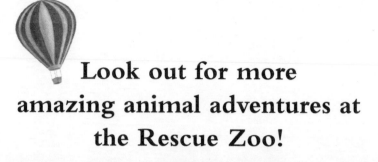

Look out for more amazing animal adventures at the Rescue Zoo!

Look out for more
of Jasmine's adventures!

Coming soon!